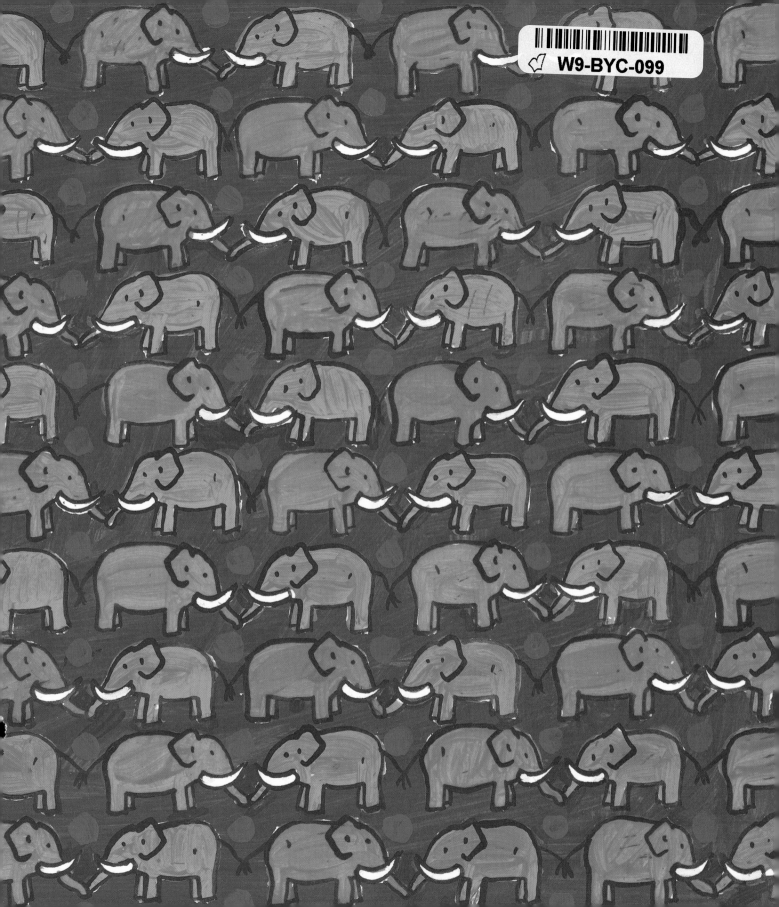

The Elephant's Child

Adapted from the story by Rudyard Kipling
Pictures by Emily Bolam

Dutton Children's Books
New York

Text adaptation copyright © 1992 by Dutton Children's Books
Illustrations copyright © 1992 by Emily Bolam

All rights reserved.

CIP Data is available.

First published in the United States 1992 by
Dutton Children's Books,
a division of Penguin Books USA Inc.

Originally published in Great Britain 1991 by Orchard Books

First American Edition   Printed in Hong Kong

10 9 8 7 6 5 4 3 2 1
ISBN 0-525-44862-4

In the High and Far-Off Times the Elephant, O Best Beloved, had no trunk. He had only a bulgy nose that he could wriggle about from side to side: but he couldn't pick up things with it.

But there was one Elephant—a new Elephant—an Elephant's Child—who was full of 'satiable curiosity, and that means he asked ever so many questions. He asked questions about everything that he saw, or heard, or felt, or smelt, or touched. He asked his tall uncle, the Giraffe, what made his skin spotty, and his tall uncle, the Giraffe, spanked him with his hard, hard hoof.

He asked his hairy uncle, the Lion, why melons tasted just so,
and his hairy uncle, the Lion, spanked him with his hairy, hairy paw.

He asked his broad aunt, the Hippopotamus, why her eyes were red, and his broad aunt, the Hippopotamus, spanked him with her broad, broad hoof. And still he was full of 'satiable curiosity!

One morning this 'satiable Elephant's Child asked a question that he had never asked before. He asked, "What does the Crocodile have for dinner?" Then everybody said "Hush!" and they spanked him immediately.

By and by, he came upon Kolokolo Bird, and he said, "My father has spanked me, and my mother has spanked me: all my aunts and uncles have spanked me for my 'satiable curiosity; and *still* I want to know what the crocodile eats for dinner!"

Then Kolokolo Bird said, with a mournful cry, "Go to the banks of the great grey-green, greasy Limpopo River, all set about with fever-trees, and find out."

That very next morning, this 'satiable Elephant's Child said to all his dear families, "Good-bye. I am going to the great grey-green, greasy Limpopo River, all set about with fever-trees, to find out what the Crocodile has for dinner."

Then he went away, and by and by came to the banks of the great grey-green, greasy Limpopo River.

Now you must understand, O Best Beloved, that this 'satiable
Elephant's Child had never seen a Crocodile till he trod on what he
thought was a log of wood at the very edge of the great grey-green,
greasy Limpopo River, all set about with fever-trees.

But it was really the Crocodile, O Best Beloved, and the
Crocodile winked one eye—like this!

"'Scuse me," said the Elephant's Child most politely, "but do you happen to have seen a Crocodile in these parts?"

The Crocodile winked the other eye and said, "Come hither, Little One, for I am the Crocodile," and he wept crocodile-tears to show it was quite true.

Then the Elephant's Child grew all breathless and said, "You are the very person I have been looking for. Will you please tell me what you have for dinner?"

"Come hither, Little One," said the Crocodile, "and I'll whisper."

Then the Elephant's Child put his head down close to the Crocodile's musky, tusky mouth, and the Crocodile caught him by his little nose.

"I think," said the Crocodile—and he said it between his teeth, like this—"I think today I will begin with Elephant's Child!"

At this, O Best Beloved, the Elephant's Child was much annoyed, and he said, speaking through his nose, like this, "Led go! You are hurtig be!" Then he sat back on his little haunches, and pulled, and pulled, and pulled, and his nose began to stretch. And the Crocodile threshed his tail like an oar, and *he* pulled, and pulled, and pulled, and at each pull the Elephant's Child's nose grew longer and longer.

But the Elephant's Child pulled hardest.

At last the Crocodile let go of the Elephant's Child's nose with a plop that you could hear all up and down the Limpopo.

Then the Elephant's Child wrapped his poor pulled nose in cool banana leaves, and hung it in the river to cool. He sat there for three days, waiting, but it never grew any shorter. For, O Best Beloved, you will understand that the Crocodile had pulled it out into a really truly trunk same as all Elephants have today. At the end of the third day, the Elephant's Child went home, frisking and whisking his new trunk.

One day he came back to all his dear families.

"O Bananas!" said they. "What have you done to your nose?"

"I got a new one from the Crocodile on the banks of the great grey-green, greasy Limpopo River," said the Elephant's Child. "I asked him what he had for dinner, and he gave me this to keep."

"It looks very ugly," said his hairy uncle, the Lion.

"It does," said the Elephant's Child. "But it's very useful," and he showed them how he could pull fruit down from a tree, instead of waiting for it to fall as he used to do.

And he showed them how he could make himself a new, cool, slushy-squshy mud-cap whenever the sun was hot.

And he showed his dear families one more thing. The Elephant's Child showed them how he could spank them all till they were very warm.

At last things grew so astonishing that his dear families went off one by one in a hurry to the banks of the great grey-green, greasy Limpopo River, all set about with fever-trees, to borrow new noses from the Crocodile.

When they came back nobody spanked anybody any more; and ever since that day, O Best Beloved, all the Elephants you will ever see, besides all those that you won't, have trunks precisely like the trunk of the 'satiable Elephant's Child.

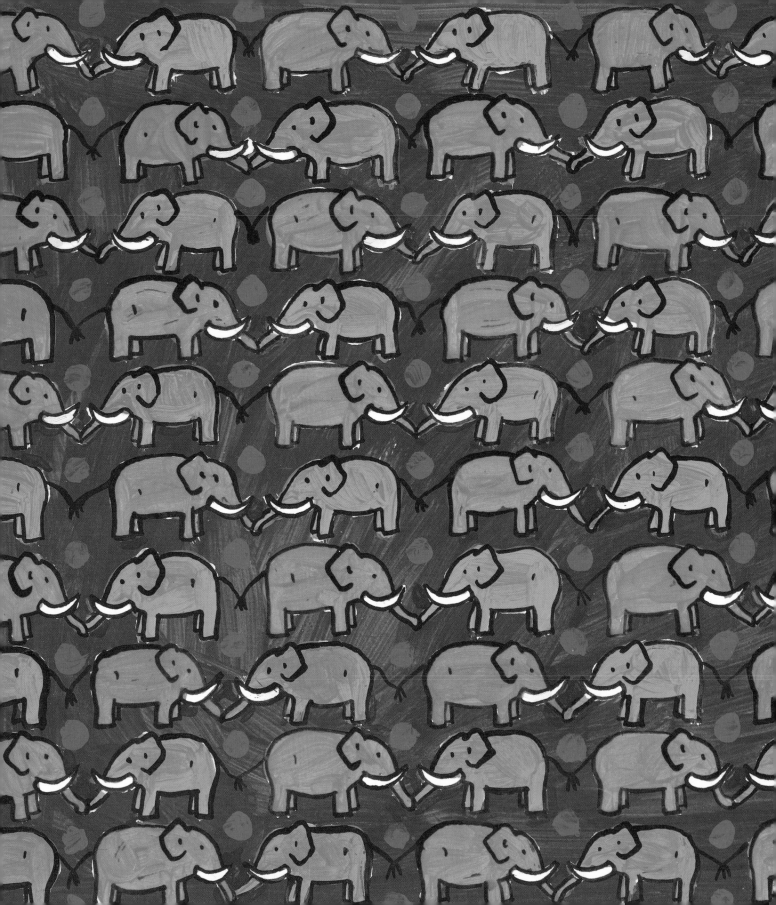